GEORGE AND MARTHA
ONE MORE TIME

For My Father

The stories in this book were originally published by Houghton Mifflin Company in *George and Martha: Rise and Shine,* 1976.

www.hmhbooks.com

First Green Light Readers edition 2011

The Library of Congress Cataloging-in-Publication Data is on file.

ISBN 978-0-547-14423-8 hardcover
ISBN 978-0-547-57689-3 paperback

Manufactured in Singapore
TWP 10 9 8 7 6 5 4 3 2 1

4500287692

Ages: 7–8
Grade: 2
Guided Reading Level: L
Reading Recovery Level: 19

GEORGE AND MARTHA ONE MORE TIME

written and illustrated by

JAMES MARSHALL

sandpiper

Green Light Readers

HOUGHTON MIFFLIN HARCOURT

BOSTON NEW YORK

STORY NUMBER ONE

THE SCARY MOVIE!

Martha was nervous.

"I've never been to a scary movie before."

"Silly goose," said George. "*Everyone* likes scary movies."

"I hope I don't faint," said Martha.

VINCENT CREEPO IN
"THE
MUMMY'S TOE"
10¢
TICKETS
5¢
M

Martha *liked* the scary movie. “This is fun,” she giggled.

Martha noticed that George was hiding under his seat.

“I’m looking for my glasses,” said George.

“You don’t wear glasses,” said Martha.

IT
EX

When the movie was over, George was as white as a sheet.

"Hold my hand," George said to Martha.

"I don't want you to be afraid walking home."

"Thank you," said Martha.

M

Story Number Two

The Secret Club

"Where are you going, George?" asked Martha.

"I'm going to my secret club," said George.

"I'll come along," said Martha.

"Oh no," said George, "it's a secret club."

"But you can let *me* in," said Martha.

"No I can't," said George. And he went on his way.

Martha was furious.

KEEP
OUT

When George was inside his secret clubhouse, Martha made a terrible fuss.

“You let me in,” she shouted.

“No,” said George.

“Yes, yes,” cried Martha.

“No, no,” said George.

“I’m coming in whether you like it or *not!*” cried Martha.

KEEP
OUT

When Martha saw the inside of George's clubhouse, she was so ashamed.

"You old sweetheart," she said to George.

George smiled. "I hope you've learned your lesson."

"I certainly have," said his friend.

THE MARTHA FAN CLUB
GEORGE, PRESIDENT
MINUTES

Answer these questions from *George and Martha: One More Time* to complete the crossword puzzle:

Across

1. Martha is afraid the scary movie will make her do this.
4. Opposite of *outside*
6. Martha feels this way before the movie.

Down

1. Martha's strong feeling toward George when he doesn't let her into his club
2. Martha's actual reaction to the movie
3. Without a doubt
5. Opposite of *over*

Unscramble the words from *George and Martha: One More Time* to fill in the blanks!

1. Martha makes a______________so that George will let her into his clubhouse. sfsu

2. George____________under his seat because the movie is too scary. diseh

3. George is the_____________of the Martha Fan Club. tnpeesidr

4. This is Martha's____________scary movie. sftir

1. fuss 2. hides 3. president 4. first

Search for these words from *George and Martha: One More Time*:

clubhouse, glasses, terrible, fan club, secret

Q	G	F	A	N	C	L	U	B	S
D	B	N	N	R	M	H	H	L	E
H	W	V	J	E	M	M	G	G	C
E	S	U	O	H	B	U	L	C	R
S	E	S	S	A	L	G	C	K	E
T	E	R	R	I	B	L	E	J	T

Q	G	F	A	N	C	L	U	B	S
D	B	N	N	R	M	H	H	L	E
H	W	V	J	E	M	M	G	G	C
E	S	U	O	H	B	U	L	C	R
S	E	S	S	A	L	G	C	K	E
T	E	R	R	I	B	L	E	J	T

Match the questions on the top with their correct answers below!

1. What is the name of George's secret club?

2. How does Martha make George feel better after the scary movie?

3. Where is George going without Martha?

4. What does Martha do to get into the clubhouse?

5. What color is George when he and Martha are walking home?

Makes a terrible fuss

As white as a sheet

Holds his hand

The Martha Fan Club

To his secret clubhouse

More Reading Practice!

Cut out flash cards on the following pages. Then practice reading the words. Sentence clues are on the back, so Mom or Dad can help and practice with you.

before

his

as

Where

let

made

"No I can't," said George.

And he went on_________way.

"I've never been to a scary movie

_________."

"_________are you going,

George?" asked Martha.

When the movie was over,

George was_________white

_________a sheet.

Martha_________a terrible fuss.

"You_________me in," she

shouted.

saw

old

Thank

When Martha________the inside of George's clubhouse, she was so ashamed.

"You________sweetheart," she said to George.

"Hold my hand," George said to Martha. "I don't want you to be afraid walking home."

"________you," said Martha.